In Times of Fire

1. NEVER HIDE UNDER BEDS OR IN CLOSETS.
   - You cannot hide from fire!

2. GET OUT FAST.
   - But don't run.

3. NEVER GO BACK FOR ANYTHING.

4. CALL THE FIRE DEPARTMENT FROM A NEIGHBOR'S HOUSE.
   - Never call from home.

5. If there's smoke:
   STAY LOW AND GO.

6. If your *clothes* catch fire:
   STOP
   DROP
   ROLL

7. FIRE FIGHTERS ARE FRIENDS.
   - Even if they sometimes look scary.

HOW COULD YOU PREVENT THE FIRE
IN THIS STORY?

Reading books
will spark your
imagination!
Mary Jessie Parker
May 1991

Erin Marie Doitchinoff
May 18, 1991
Young Authors Conference
Normal, IL.

Night Fire!

by Mary Jessie Parker
Illustrated by Lynne Dennis

SCHOLASTIC INC. • New York

Night comes.

Sparks leap.
Papers smolder.

Flames spread.

Fire grows.
Flames blaze.

Smoke spreads.
Alarm buzzes.

Dog barks.
Cat howls.

Children wake.
They sniff.

Children call.
Parents come.

They hurry.

They're safe.
They knock.

Neighbors wake.
They call.

They wait.

Bells clang.
Fire fighters dress.
Engines roar.

Sirens shriek.
Help comes.

Fire fighters work.
Water pours. People gather.

Some watch.
Some cry.

Fire's out.
Engines leave.

All are safe.

Friends help.

For James, Ida Jennie,
and Elizabeth
— M.J.P. —

In honor of
731 Brooks Avenue
— L.D. —

We gratefully acknowledge Joseph F. Bruno,
Fire Commissioner of the New York City Fire Department;
Joseph E. Spinnato, former Fire Commissioner of
the New York City Fire Department; Marilyn R. Bernard,
Special Projects Director of the New York City
Fire Department; and Eddie Bain,
Director of Public Education and Information
of the Champaign, Illinois, Fire Department
for their guidance in the preparation
of this book.

Text copyright © 1989 by Mary Jessie Parker.
Illustrations copyright © 1989 by Lynne Dennis.
All rights reserved. Published by Scholastic Inc.
SCHOLASTIC HARDCOVER is a registered trademark of Scholastic Inc.
730 Broadway, New York, N.Y. 10003.
Design by Claire Counihan.

Cataloging-in-Publication data available
Library of Congress number: 86-31748
ISBN 0-590-41423-2

12 11 10 9 8 7 6 5 4 3 2 1   9/8 0 1 2 3/9
Printed in the U.S.A.   36
First Scholastic Printing, November 1989

KEEP SAFE FROM FIRE

Plan Ahead

1. MAKE SURE THE FIRE IN THE FIREPLACE
   IS COMPLETELY OUT AT NIGHT.

   - Always have fireplace screens or doors
     closed when there is a fire there.

2. PLAN A SAFE FIRE ESCAPE ROUTE WITH
   YOUR FAMILY.

   - Find some different routes, in case one is
     blocked by smoke or fire.

   - Have practice drills using all of your
     different routes.

3. EVERY ROOM SHOULD HAVE A SMOKE DETECTOR.

   - Batteries need to be changed once a year.

   - Pets will make sounds when they smell
     smoke. But a smoke detector will tell you long
     before a pet will.

4. KEEP A WHISTLE BY YOUR BED.

   - It will help you call at night.

5. NEVER PLAY WITH MATCHES OR FIRE.